OUT OF THIS WORLD

Rigby, Halley Court, Jordan Hill, Oxford, OX2 8EJ
a division of Reed Educational and Professional Publishing Ltd
www.rigbyed.co.uk

Rigby is a registered trademark of Reed Educational and Professional
Publishing Ltd

Out of this World first published 2002

'The Charms of Earth' © Michael Lawrence 2002
'Baby Steps' © Paul Shipton 2002
'YouthLab 2030' © Lesley Howarth 2002

Series editor: Wendy Wren

06 05 04
10 9 8 7 6 5 4

Out of this World   ISBN 0433 07748 4
Group Reading Pack with Teaching Notes   ISBN 0433 07754 9

Illustrated by Andy Warrington, Dylan Coburn, Lorenzo Van Der Lingen
Cover illustration © Philip Nicholson / Thorogood Illustration 2002
Repro by Digital Imaging, Glasgow
Printed in Great Britain by Ashford Colour Press, Gosport, Hants.

THE CHARMS OF EARTH
by Michael Lawrence

There was once a small, blue planet called Earth. Most of the people of Earth were as ordinary as can be – Dodi and Maurice Platt, for instance. Dodi and Maurice had a fine little home and were comfortably off. Maurice owned a doughnut shop in the High Street, and Dodi spent as much time as she could in the garden. At the end of every day, they both liked to relax in front of the television.

They were relaxing in front of it
one spring evening, when they heard
something on the news that was to change
their lives completely.

"Scientists have discovered," said the
newscaster, "that the world's core has been
heating up. Within six calendar months,
the Earth will be so hot it will explode."

"Explode?" Dodi said. "What does he
mean, explode?"

"He means 'go bang', dear," explained
Maurice. "Blow up."

"Oh, I don't like the sound of that.
It'll ruin my garden."

The newscaster went on to say that the world's governments had decided that the planet must be evacuated. An escape committee, called ESCOM for short, had been set up to design and build the spacecraft that would send the people of Earth into space to look for another home.

"Does that mean I'll have to leave my garden?" wailed Dodi.

"I think you might," said Maurice.

"Change the channel, dear. This is so depressing."

Next morning, Maurice Platt went to his shop. He was about to open up for the day, when he remembered that the world was going to end.

"What's the point?" he sighed. "The world's going to end. I'm not going to spend my last six months on Earth selling doughnuts."

Instead of opening the shop, he took down the big plastic ring doughnut fixed above the door and hurled it into the air. Then he went home.

The spinning doughnut zoomed up and up. It caught the eye of a young man called Steve Lively, who was passing on his way to work.

Steve Lively was a brilliant aeronautical engineer who'd been given the task of designing a fleet of spacecraft to carry the population of Earth to another planet. Steve was worried. He would have welcomed such a challenge if he'd had two or three years to work on it. The trouble was, he only had a few months and he didn't know where to start. When he saw Maurice fling his plastic doughnut into the air, Steve just stared. The doughnut was going so fast, and so far, that it looked as if it would reach the sun.

"That's it!" he cried. "Spacecraft shaped like ring doughnuts! They'll spin round the hole in the middle and keep on spinning, as long as nothing gets in their way. Fire them at the sun and the solar winds will fling them into deep space!"

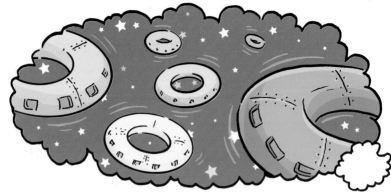

Steve was so excited by the idea that, instead of going to the office, he rushed round the corner to share it with his girlfriend, Anna. She was a painter and, when she heard the space-doughnut plan, her eyes lit up.

"Steve!" she cried. "The doughnuts can be all the colours of the rainbow!"

"Anna," Steve said, patiently, "this isn't an idea for a painting! It's a brilliant plan for saving the people of Earth from being blown to smithereens."

Anna immediately went into a sulk. Steve sighed. He never could stand up to Anna's sulks.

"I'll see what I can do," he said, wearily. He took his multi-coloured flying doughnut plan to ESCOM. At first the committee was not too sure about it.

"You say the doughnuts will spin round and round as they fly through space," one committee member said. "Won't the passengers get dizzy?"

"No, no," Steve assured him. "The passengers will spin with the doughnut, so the space they occupy will be perfectly still. To them everything outside will seem to be moving."

"How would we launch these spinning doughnuts?" another committee member enquired.

"Giant catapults," said Steve. He had dreamed this up on the way to the meeting and was very pleased with himself.

"Why all the different colours?" asked someone else.

"So that we can tell them apart, of course," Steve replied.

The committee was satisfied. The order was given to build ten thousand multi-coloured, doughnut-shaped spacecraft and a thousand giant catapults to fire them.

During the next four months the planet's surface grew hotter and hotter. Cracks appeared in the streets. Trees sank into the ground. Seas began to steam and bubble. Scientists warned that, if the space doughnuts were not ready in six or seven weeks, everyone would perish. The plan had been to wait until all the doughnuts were finished before launching them, but ESCOM now decided to launch them, one by one, as they came off the production line.

The people of Earth were getting very jittery by this time, so when the first doughnut was ready there was a mad scramble to get on board.

The first doughnut (which was an amazing shade of pink) was loaded into one of the giant catapults and fired at the sun. Telescopes, binoculars and news cameras followed it, so that the entire world could see how it got on. The watchers held their breath, but not half as much as the passengers on the pink doughnut. For all they knew, they were about to plunge into the sun's fiery heart and be turned to toast.

They need not have worried. Everything worked perfectly. The solar winds caught the doughnut and hurled it out of the solar system into deep space. Steve Lively's idea was a success! Within days, doughnuts of every hue were being catapulted into space.

Steve was proud of his achievement, but there was one thing that bothered him. Once a doughnut was on its way, there was no telling where it would end up. He didn't want to alarm anyone, however, so he kept his worries to himself.

Unlike Steve, Anna had no worries. She was very happy. The multi-coloured doughnuts, shooting one after another into space like fistfuls of gleaming jewels, had made her famous. Reporters from newspapers and magazines wanted to interview her and take her picture. Anna loved the attention, but Steve was annoyed.

Anna was so full of herself now. He was really going off her.

The day came when all but one doughnut had been launched. Most of the passengers on the last doughnut were very modest people who didn't like to push themselves forward – people like Dodi and Maurice Platt. Maurice had no idea that he had started all this by flinging his plastic doughnut into the air.

The planet was now too hot to walk on. All vegetation had died. Towns and cities had crumbled. Even the oceans had dried up, apart from the odd salty puddle, leaving the steaming seabeds littered with griddled fish.

"It was a fine world," Steve Lively said as he set the timer that would catapult the last doughnut towards the sun. He walked sadly up the gangplank and closed the airlock. The only thing he was happy about was that he had persuaded Anna to leave on an earlier doughnut. With any luck, they would end up on different planets!

The catapult fired the last doughnut, which was purple, towards the sun. It was about half way there when the Earth exploded. Shortly afterwards, the solar winds caught the doughnut and blew it into deep space.

"I do miss my garden," said Dodi Platt, two minutes later.

Time passed.

A lot of time.

Every now and then, the purple doughnut would approach another sun, whose solar winds would spin it towards the next, and so on. The passengers on the purple doughnut eventually got used to travelling through a galaxy of spinning stars, and ceased to get dizzy when looking out of the portholes. They looked out constantly, hoping to see other doughnuts, but they never did. It was as if they were quite alone in the vast expanse of space. Occasionally, they came across a planet that, from a distance, looked as if it might suit them, but closer inspection always showed that it was too hot, or too cold, or the atmosphere was wrong, so they continued on their way.

One day they chanced upon a planet that bore a striking resemblance to their own Earth. It was quite a bit bigger, but that didn't matter. They made all the usual tests from space and found that the conditions were perfect. The purple doughnut entered the planet's atmosphere and descended towards the surface. Soon the passengers saw, far below, towns and cities and roads.

"Civilisation!" they cried.

"That means gardens!" said Dodi Platt.

"Give me strength!" groaned Maurice.

Suddenly the craft lurched sharply. Voices rose in panic.

"What was that? What's happening?"

"Electrical storm, I think!" Steve said. "Get to your seats! Strap yourselves in!" Everyone strapped themselves in as lightning flashed across the portholes.

Down the doughnut tumbled, down and down. The passengers moaned and cried. They were doomed, doomed! Suddenly, there was a great jolt, followed by a mighty roaring sound. The view from the portholes showed that they had not hit the ground at all. They had plunged into deep water.

"I didn't think we were over an ocean," Steve said, puzzled.

The doughnut began to rise in the water. Up and up it climbed, until it bobbed on the surface. Sunlight poured in. People unstrapped themselves, hardly able to believe they were still alive.

"We've made it!" someone said. "We've found our new home!"

"What a pity our people aren't here to share it with us," sighed someone else.

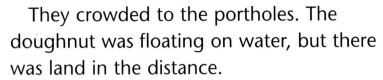

They crowded to the portholes. The doughnut was floating on water, but there was land in the distance.

"Hello, what's that thing coming towards us?" said Maurice.

Everyone peered.

"It looks like. . . a hand."

"Pretty big for a hand."

A hand it was, though. A hand like any one of theirs, but a thousand times larger. The owner of the hand, a female, was similarly huge.

"Another one!" she cried, plucking the tiny purple ring from the water and drying it on her hanky. "Where on *Earth* do they keep coming from?"

The enormous woman unclasped the charm bracelet that encircled her wrist. She threaded it through the hole in the middle of the doughnut from outer space. She closed the clasp and held her wrist aloft. The sun glinted on the dozens of identical but differently coloured charms she had been collecting since they started appearing in her swimming pool. Then she leaned back in her deckchair, adjusted her sunhat, and went to sleep.

Steve, Dodi, Maurice and the others pressed their noses against the portholes. Faces peered back at them from the next doughnut, a green one, on the chain round the woman's wrist. Some of the faces were familiar – one in particular. She was waving, madly.

"Steve!" she shouted.

BABY STEPS

by Paul Shipton

It was a perfect day. Birdsong played over the speakers, and the ceiling of every level in the City was a deep, deep blue. The people on the Level 67 Walker Belt were all riding towards the Vid-Games Court. They chatted excitedly about high scores and strategies for the games they planned to play. Only Bean was silent.

Everyone in the City had somewhere to go and something fun to do. Mother made sure of that. Some (mostly Oldies) entered the Bingo Zone. Other citizens got ready for Blast Ball in the Sports Zone. Toddlers crowded into the Watch-With-Mother Zone.

At the Vid-Games Court, Bean waited until it was his turn to talk to Mother.

"Hello, Mother," he said to the screen.

"Hello, Bean," Mother's smile was warm. Bean knew every bit of her computer-generated face. "What are you going to play today?"

"Erm. . . " Under Mother's gaze, the names slipped from Bean's mind. A look of concern filled Mother's digital eyes. "What's wrong, Bean?"

"I'm fine," Bean answered quickly. The thing was, he didn't really want to play any vid-games but how could he tell Mother that? After all, Mother let everyone in the City do whatever they wanted. How could he explain that he didn't want to do anything?

At last he plucked out a name. "I'll play *Attack on Planet Delta*," he said.

Mother smiled. "Good choice! Go to door 16, Bean."

Bean followed the trail of footprints that showed the way but half-way there he gave a quick look over his shoulder. Sure that no one was watching, he jumped off the belt and dashed up a staircase. He hurried into a dead-end corridor and crouched low. No one would follow him in here. Only repair robots came into this kind of place.

From this spot, he could look down on the crowd milling around in the brightly lit Vid-Games Court. Their faces shone with happy anticipation of the day's games. Mother made sure everyone in the City was happy. So what's wrong with me? Bean asked himself. Why don't I feel happy? Why am I different?

SERVICE ONLY

He'd asked these questions many times but there was never an answer. Then something happened that swept all thoughts away. A hole in the world opened up! A metal wall-panel at the end of his secret corridor fell to the floor with a clang. And then a man clambered through.

He was old, but he didn't look like the Oldies in the Bingo Zone. His grey hair was long and he had a wild, bushy beard. His clothes were shabby. There was only one explanation. This was an Outie – someone from outside the City! Bean had heard about them, but he'd never seen one before.

The intruder strode down into the Vid-Games Court with a big grin. Everyone noticed him immediately, especially when the man threw back his head in a great booming laugh.

"You always know where Gramps is," chuckled a voice by Bean's ear. "Just listen for his laugh."

Bean gasped. A girl – another Outie – was standing right next to him!

"I'm Jenna," she grinned. "Who are you?"

"Bean. But how did you. . . ?"

"Get here? I followed Gramps."

"But you're Outies!" Bean exclaimed.

Jenna laughed. "Actually, it was easy. Gramps says that we could come and go any time. Most Outies aren't interested, but Gramps is different. He used to live here."

Bean glanced down at the man. He was pointing at the walls and talking loudly to the small crowd around him. "You mean he was an Innie?"

Jenna nodded. "Years ago, yes. But we don't call you Innies."

"What do you call us?"

"We call you the Babies."

"Why do. . . ?" Bean didn't have time to finish his question. Something was happening below.

"What's that?" gasped Jenna, as a robot bleeped fiercely at the old man.

"That's a Dad-Bot," Bean explained.

The crowd let the robot through.

"You are an intruder," growled the face on the Dad-Bot's chest screen. Gramps held out his open hands. "You've got me!" he laughed. A squiggle of light crackled out from the robot and wrapped around Gramps' wrists. The silent crowd watched as the Dad-Bot led the intruder away.

"Gramps said this would happen," said Jenna. "They're taking him outside." Her voice was anxious now. Suddenly there was another fierce bleep, closer this time. It was a second Dad-Bot and it was coming their way!

There was no time to think. Bean found himself grabbing Jenna's arm.

"This way!" he hissed. They pelted along a narrow service walkway and down into the Games Court. Pushing their way through the crowd, they reached the Slider down to the level below.

"Stop!" called a robotic voice, but they were already sliding down. On Level 66 they elbowed their way through a crowd laughing at a cartoon. The cartoon figures towered as high as the ceiling.

As they ran, Bean kept glancing back. The Dad-Bot was still chasing them, its screen-face set to angry. They had to be fast. There was a small alcove set into the wall of this corridor. Bean pulled Jenna into it and they crouched behind the air unit. Seconds later, the Dad-Bot zoomed right by without stopping.

It took them a while to catch their breath, then Jenna asked, "How did you know this place was here?"

Bean shrugged. "There are lots of secret places like this in the City. Most people don't even notice them, but I do. Sometimes I just like to sit on my own." He looked into Jenna's eyes. "Now, you tell me – why do you call us the Babies?"

Jenna's expression was serious. "Well," she said carefully, "you don't do anything for yourselves, do you? You don't work, you don't make your food or even bring up your kids. You just play all day."

Bean nodded slowly.

"Gramps says we should be sorry for you," continued Jenna. "He says that years ago machines got cleverer and cleverer. . . so clever they could make new machines that were cleverer still. The machines started doing all the work. Now the City is one big network of machines. Mother is the computer that controls it all. She does everything for you – including thinking." Jenna looked around at the walls and ceiling of Level 66. "But Gramps just wasn't happy here. Life was easy and everything was done for him, but there was something missing. . . do you understand?"

Bean did. He felt as if Jenna were describing his own feelings.

"But what's it like on the outside?" he asked.

"Well, it isn't perfect, of course. . . " Jenna indicated the City around them with a wave. "But it's better than all of this. It's just *real*."

"How do you mean, real?"

Jenna furrowed her brow in concentration, then asked, "Have you ever seen an animal?"

"Well, there's Bomba and Goonie in the Cartoon Zone. Bomba's this stupid cat who. . . "

"No, I mean real, living, breathing animals."

Bean shook his head.

Jenna sighed in frustration. "How can I explain things you don't know the first thing about? Real trees and real flowers, a sky full of stars instead of a ceiling always over your head. . . " These words didn't mean much to Bean but he felt his heart stir with excitement.

Jenna stopped and reached into her bag. "Here," she said. "Eat this. It's an apple."

Bean looked at the lumpy green thing with its dull, bruised skin.

"Go on," urged Jenna.

The apple felt good and solid in Bean's hand. As he sniffed it he saw Jenna's smile freeze on her face. He turned and saw a Dad-Bot.

"Come with me, intruder," commanded the face on the chest screen.

Jenna stood up slowly. There was no point in running.

"See you, Bean," she said with a brave wink. The Dad-Bot began to lead her away.

"But wait! I want to know more about life outside! I have to. . . "

"That's easy," called Jenna over her shoulder. "Go and see for yourself."

And then she was gone.

Bean didn't hide again that morning. He played a vid-game but it wasn't as exciting as running from the Dad-Bot. He couldn't stop thinking about the Outies or about what Jenna had said.

When the lunch bell chimed, he joined a queue at a food station. He shuffled forward to the feeder tubes. The choice today was red or green mush. Bean chose green and Mother squirted the food into his plastic bowl.

Suddenly an angry voice shouted from the Food Station. "Mother, it's not fair. She's got more than me!" A man was pointing crossly to the bowl held by the woman next to him.

"Have not!" snapped the woman.

"Have too!" yelled the man. His face was red and scrunched up like a big baby.

Bean turned away. Then he remembered the apple. He took it from his pocket, lifted it to his lips and bit. It was incredible, like nothing he'd ever known. The taste seemed to fizz all over his tongue. He ate it quickly, core and all.

Bean looked glumly at his bowl of bright green mush. He couldn't eat this now. And that's when he knew it. He was going to leave the City.

He hurried back to the corridor on Level 67. The metal panel was in its place again, but it wasn't hard to pull open. Almost immediately, a Dad-Bot appeared by his side. The chest screen flickered and Mother's smile appeared.

"What are you doing, Bean?" she asked.

"I'm leaving."

"Will you come back?"

"I. . . don't know."

Mother was silent. Then, "Goodbye, Bean," she said.

He stepped into the opening. The dark corridor was filled with machinery and wires. Bean kept on walking until he found an elevator shaft. The long ride took him down to ground level. Finally he came to a metal hatch.

He pushed it open slowly and for the first time in his life, he stepped outside the City. The air rushed against him, harder than any blast from an air vent. Bean felt as if he might lift off into the limitless blue above him.

He was scared but excited, too. He looked back once at the City. The huge rectangle towered up into the clouds. Its many levels were the world to thousands of people. But not to him. The real world was waiting.

"Goodbye, Mother!" he shouted. Then he ran towards a line of real trees in the distance.

YouthLab 2030

by Lesley Howarth

"So what will you do on Mars Station?" my sister Emma had asked.

"Experiments," I told her. "Mind and body."

"But what will you actually *do*?" she asked, again.

"Someone has to explore new worlds."

"Why do they?" Emma asked.

"Because no one ever got anywhere without exploring new things."

"So when you're on Mars station— "

"I'll look after the food. Twilight Replenisher's my job title. I'll grow plants and yeasts to feed the team. See that the shelves are stacked with supplies," I said.

"But what will you do the rest of the time?"

"I'll write you letters," I had told her, before I left. "I'm on my way any day now, and I won't get back for over three years."

My name's Callum Williams – I'm on the YouthLab Mission to Mars. We slept on the spaceflight out. Eighteen months we spent in space before we woke up and saw the red rocks of Mars through our window.

We left the space-shuttle and went out into the dust storm in our space-suits. A few steps brought us to the airlock which shut out the Mars atmosphere and made Mars Station a comfortable place to live. It was made up of the Living Pod, for humans, and the Grow Pod, for plants.

My job, as I said before, was to see that we had plenty of food. If we couldn't show that we could look after ourselves, that bean plants could sprout on Mars, for example, then that would be the end of all Mars missions. It was a really important job, and we all had a part in it.

George Turner's job was Systems Engineer. Kidman was the Captain. My job was Twilight Replenisher. No one supervised us. We supervised ourselves.

You had to be at least nine years old to take part in the YouthLab Mission. The purpose of YouthLab was to test young people's long-term reactions in space, with a view to a permanent settlement. A whole town, where everyone would be ten – just how weird would that be? Other teams had been selected for flight duty as well but we were the only team to blast off.

We worked well together, but soon George began acting strangely. The first sign was talking in his sleep.

"Home!" he shouted. "Jamie! Mum! DAD!" I worked at night so I had to be careful not to disturb him. It only made his sleep-talking worse. I had to check the water recycling, pick mushrooms, soak beans, feed the guinea pigs, check on the yeasts and stack the shelves with food for the next day, while Kidman and George slept. Any time I had left, I wrote letters home. I couldn't email or make contact by computer. Even space-age technology couldn't cope with an eighteen-month time-lag. We were on our own at Mars Station, the loneliest place in the galaxy.

One night, George started sleepwalking and something awful happened. I wrote to my sister Emma about it.

Dear Em,

Guess what? George went outside last night in the dust storm without a space-suit! Kidman went out after him. I paid out the oxygen line, and we only just got him back.

I've got you a Mission patch. You can have it when I get back. It's cool. Three kids on the surface of Mars. Around the edge it says: 'Mars YouthLab 2030– KIDMAN–TURNER– WILLIAMS'. I was lucky to find a spare one. I'm keeping it in my locker for you.

Pity this letter won't reach you before I do. Think George will be glad to get home.

Hope Henry's OK. Give him a bone from me!

I'll know if you've been in my room while I've been away – so don't even think about it!

Cal

"George, why did you do it?" Kidman asked, the next morning.

"Why did I do what?" George said.

"You went outside last night, remember?" Kidman reminded him. "We dragged you back. You might have died. What did you think you were doing?"

"I don't know," George said. "I want to go home."

"We have ways to deal with that," Kidman said, giving George an Emergency Home Package. These packages were provided for life-threatening homesickness. George's was life-threatening all right. He might have killed us all that night. He ripped open the package with trembling hands. "Lollies." He held up a big, red, sticky lolly the size of a saucer. "Mittens, an electronic game, a hat, a book, and a 'Smell From Home' in a bag. Pooh! Liquorice, isn't it?"

I smelled the bag. "Smells like a bus shelter." I smelled it again. "Remember bus shelters, don't you?"

I went to my bunk and slept so I had no idea what George did for the rest of that day. But the next night, when I was refilling shelves, I had to pass George to get something. As I crept past his bunk, he reached out and grabbed my ankle.

"Escape!" he shouted. "Home!"

"George," I said, "you're dreaming. Let go." But I couldn't get his hand off my leg.

"Tomorrow," he said. "You and me."

"Tomorrow we'll talk about it." At last his hand relaxed.

I crept along to Kidman's bunk. "Kidman! Wake up!"

"What is it?" Kidman asked.

"You know George is going to crack, don't you," I warned her through the darkness. "Major danger to the Mission."

"Get him to send out Rover," Kidman yawned. "Give him something to do."

Rover was the remote-controlled vehicle we could send out to pick up stones. You could go for a 'walk' and look at the Mars-scape through the cameras in its 'eyes'.

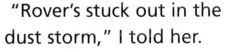

"Rover's stuck out in the dust storm," I told her.

"What do you expect me to do about it?" Kidman was always polite.

"Return shuttle's due in a month. Eighteen months to get home. Till then, George copes."

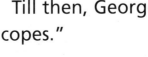

But the next day he didn't cope.
Instead George roamed around the pod,
whingeing about the food. "Where's the
yeast extract?" he grumbled.

"The Marsmite?"
I pointed it out. "Behind
the canned rhubarb.
I filled it up last night."

George helped
himself, then slouched
back to his seat.

"Get some exercise,"
I suggested. "At least do
some experiments.
Someone has to try out
the inflatable trousers."

The inflatable trousers
forced blood from your legs to your trunk,
to help it to circulate in weakened gravity.
We were meant to record the effect while
doing different exercises.

"Try 'em yourself," George grunted.

"I'm going to sleep now, remember?"
I told him. "*You* work during the day."

The dust storm outside seemed to batter Mars Station all that day, feeling for any weakness, trying to find a hole in its skin. The tiniest hole in the pods, and all the oxygen would rush out and we would suffocate in moments, before we could reach our space-suits. A Mars day was a little longer than an Earth day. That Tuesday it seemed like a century but I must have slept at last.

"Cal," said a voice through the darkness.

I opened my eyes. "What time is it?"

George's eyes stared into mine. "Time we were out of here."

"Thanks for waking me up," I said. "Almost late for work!"

"The Grow Pod— home— " George sounded funny.

I jumped up and looked around. I could see that the Grow Pod next door had de-pressurised. Its walls sagged against the Living Pod walls, with no atmosphere to hold them out. They thrashed to and fro in the dust storm, threatening to make a hole in the Living Pod walls.

"George," I said, "what did you do?"

"I let the vegetables go home."

"You opened the Grow Pod airlock?"

"They wanted to go," George said.

I jumped up and checked the airlock in the Living Pod. Keep calm, I said to myself. The Grow Pod airlock was open and the vegetables had frozen or exploded, but so long as the Living Pod stayed intact, we still had a chance to survive. Luckily the water-recycling plant was inside the Living Pod. How much did that leave us to eat?

"We have yeasts, guinea pigs and mushrooms," I said. "What else?"

"Ice-cream at home," George murmured. "Eighteen months to get back. I'll be old by the time I get home."

"You'll be twelve," I reminded him. "Don't wake Kidman, all right? Kidman won't understand. But me and you, we can make it."

I made him fetch the Home Package Kidman had given him the other day. He put on the fluffy mittens while I searched for something useful. They put things in every Home Package for smell, touch, body and mind. A packet of flower seeds fell out of the hat. Not much hope we'd be able to grow them now, but I planted them anyway. Marigold and Forget-me-not, Pansy and Love-in-a-Mist. Just the names made me feel better.

"Look," George said, "no hands." He was pleased with his soft, woolly mittens.

"No brain," I joked back, wondering how we could have let this happen.

Early the next morning we replenished the shelves together with what was left in the Living Pod.

"We can make it, can't we?" said George. "Do without vegetables, I mean?"

"Kings of Mars, aren't we?" I said. I could see how worried he was.

"There's a force-field out there," he told me.

"What are you talking about?" I asked.

"Outside," he said. "When you rescued me. Something stopped me from going any further."

What did he mean? "Stay away from the Living Pod airlock," I warned George, anyway. "Open it once, and we're dead."

"Haven't been anywhere near it," he said. "It's Kidman you want to watch. Kidman," he said, "she's not well."

My heart did a double-flip. "You didn't ... let her go home?" I rushed to wake her. "Kidman, wake up, what's wrong?"

"Get off me." Kidman turned over.

"She sleeps all the time," George said.

What with working at night, I suppose I hadn't noticed. Now I couldn't wake her. George spent his time trying to unjam Rover, still stuck outside. The side of the Living Pod attached to the Grow Pod was starting to freeze. Soon it would slowly leak. Oxygen levels were dropping already.

There was only one thing to do.

It was against the rules to open the last Emergency Home Package, the one that was labelled *OPEN ONLY WHEN MISSION ABOUT TO ABORT*, without the rest of the crew's agreement, but I did it anyway. Inside, there was a button. I pressed it and the airlock cracked open. I jumped up. "Oh, no!" I cried as the Mars atmosphere rushed in.

"Nice training run. Good team skills in what could have been a real situation," said a voice from overhead.

I was back at Mission Control!

"You mean we never left Earth?"

"But lift-off?" George said.

"So long in space?"

The Chief Technician laughed. "We sent you to sleep for three days, I'm afraid."

"The desert outside?" asked Kidman.

"Faked with a dust-machine in a tank."

"I did everything right," Kidman said. "It was Cal who broke the rules."

"Cal's the only one who'll be on the Mars Mission next Spring," the Chief said.

"He helped me," George said.

"Cal stayed focussed in an emergency," the Chief said. "And he planted flowers."

"Flowers are no use, they're just pretty," said Kidman.

"Exactly," the Chief agreed.

Kidman rubbed her eyes. "He can go. I don't care."

"Actually— " I stripped off my Mission patch. "I think I just landed on Earth."